JP DON
Donaldson, Julia.
Welcome to the world   **WH**

FEB - 6 2023

D1467745

WELCOME
TO THE WORLD

Julia Donaldson
Illustrated by Helen Oxenbury

A Paula Wiseman Book
Simon & Schuster Books for Young Readers
New York   London   Toronto   Sydney   New Delhi

3 3281 02159 879 9

Welcome to the world.
Welcome to the light.

Welcome to the day.

Welcome to the night.

Welcome to your mommy.
Welcome to your feeds.
Welcome to the earrings
and the buttons and the beads.

Welcome to a pair of eyes,
a smiling mouth, a nose.

Welcome to your fingers.
Welcome to your toes.

Welcome to the grass. Welcome to the trees.

Welcome to the doorbell
and the jingling of the keys.

Welcome to the cows.
Welcome to the sheep.

Welcome to the lullabies
that send you off to sleep.

Welcome to the sounds.
Welcome to the shapes.
Welcome to the strawberries,
the apples, and the grapes.

Welcome to the colors
    yellow, red, and blue.
And the person in the mirror
    who looks a bit like you.

Welcome to the clouds.
Welcome to the swing.
Welcome to the little birds
that hop and peck and sing.

Welcome to your granny's knees
  that bounce you up and down.
Welcome to the buses
  rumbling round the town.

Welcome to the bicycles. Welcome to the cars.

Welcome to the granddads
strumming their guitars.

Welcome to your bathtub
with the towels and the tiles.

Welcome to the songs and rhymes,
the stories and the smiles.

Welcome to the ladybugs.
Welcome to the snails.

The cats that arch their furry backs,
the dogs that wag their tails.

Welcome to the ducks.
Welcome to the swans.

Welcome to the café
with the coffee
and the scones.

Welcome to the girls.
Welcome to the boys.

Welcome to your teddies.
Welcome to your toys.

Welcome to the daisies.
Welcome to the roses.

Welcome to the glasses
    that are fun to pull off noses.

Welcome to the bubbles
that shine and then go pop.

Welcome to the pushcart
 and the rides around the shop.

Welcome to the candles,
    the cups and plates and spoons.
Welcome to bananas.
    Welcome to balloons.

Welcome to the pinwheels
    in the windy weather.
Welcome to the babies
    who will all grow up together.

Welcome to the earth below
and to the sky above.

Welcome, little baby.
Welcome to our love.

To baby Arthur and his big brother, Henry – J. D.
To little Bonnie and her big sister, Lily, and brother, Charlie,
and to Nell and Woody too – H. O.

SIMON & SCHUSTER BOOKS FOR YOUNG READERS
An imprint of Simon & Schuster Children's Publishing Division
1230 Avenue of the Americas, New York, New York 10020
Text © 2022 by Julia Donaldson
Illustration © 2022 by Helen Oxenbury
Originally published in Great Britain in 2022 by Penguin Random House UK
All rights reserved, including the right of reproduction in whole or in part in any form.
SIMON & SCHUSTER BOOKS FOR YOUNG READERS
and related marks are trademarks of Simon & Schuster, Inc.
For information about special discounts for bulk purchases, please contact Simon &
Schuster Special Sales at 1-866-506-1949 or business@simonandschuster.com.
The Simon & Schuster Speakers Bureau can bring authors to your live event.
For more information or to book an event, contact the Simon & Schuster Speakers Bureau
at 1-866-248-3049 or visit our website at www.simonspeakers.com.
The text for this book was set in Alice.
The illustrations for this book were rendered in pencil line, watercolor, and gouache.
Manufactured in China
0422 PUK
First US edition January 2023
2 4 6 8 10 9 7 5 3 1
CIP data for this book is available from the Library of Congress.
ISBN 9781665929875
ISBN 9781665929882 (ebook)